12/17/21

I0623733

12 Days of Christmas

Random House New York

This BOOK belongs to:

The Plan:
Build
Eat
Play
Stay up all night
See Santa

On the **FIRST** day of Christmas,

My best friend gave to me . . .

Some cookies for **SANTA** to eat.

For
Santa

On the **SECOND** day of Christmas,

My best friend gave to me . . .

2 Christmas stockings,

And some cookies for **SANTA** to eat.

For Santa

On the THIRD day of Christmas,

My best friend gave to me . . .

3 shiny buttons,

2 Christmas stockings,

And some cookies for SANTA to eat.

On the **FOURTH** day of Christmas,
My best friend gave to me . . .

4 mugs of cocoa,

3 shiny buttons,
2 Christmas stockings,
And some cookies for **SANTA** to eat.

On the **FIFTH** day of Christmas,
My best friend gave to me . . .

4 mugs of cocoa,
3 shiny buttons,
2 Christmas stockings,
And some cookies for **SANTA** to eat.

On the SIXTH day of Christmas,
My best friend gave to me . . .

6 skaters skating,

5 donut rings . . .
4 mugs of cocoa,
3 shiny buttons,
2 Christmas stockings,
And some cookies for SANTA to eat.

On the SEVENTH day of Christmas,

My best friend gave to me . . .

7 robots dancing,

6 skaters skating,

5 donut rings . . .

4 mugs of cocoa,

3 shiny buttons,

2 Christmas stockings,

And some cookies for SANTA to eat.

On the EIGHTH day of Christmas,
My best friend gave to me . . .

8 pirates playing,

7 robots dancing,
6 skaters skating,
5 donut rings . . .
4 mugs of cocoa,
3 shiny buttons,
2 Christmas stockings,
And some cookies for SANTA to eat.

On the NINTH day of Christmas,
My best friend gave to me . . .

9 reindeer flying,

8 pirates playing,
7 robots dancing,
6 skaters skating,
5 donut rings . . .
4 mugs of cocoa,
3 shiny buttons,
2 Christmas stockings,
And some cookies for SANTA to eat.

On the TENTH day of Christmas,
My best friend gave to me . . .

10 train cars chugging,

9 reindeer flying,
8 pirates playing,
7 robots dancing,
6 skaters skating,
5 donut rings . . .

4 mugs of cocoa,
3 shiny buttons,
2 Christmas stockings,
And some cookies for SANTA to eat.

On the ELEVENTH day of Christmas,

My best friend gave to me . . .

11 fairies sparkling,

10 train cars chugging,

9 reindeer flying,

8 pirates playing,

7 robots dancing,

6 skaters skating,

5 donut rings . . .

4 mugs of cocoa,

3 shiny buttons,

2 Christmas stockings,

And some cookies for SANTA to eat.

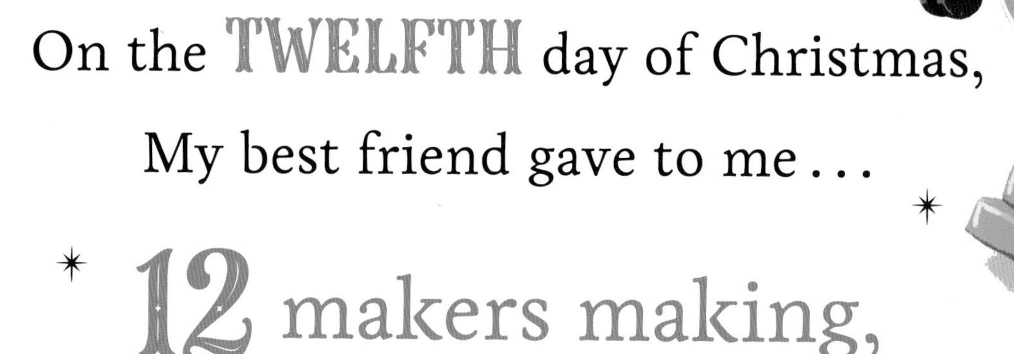

On the TWELFTH day of Christmas,
My best friend gave to me . . .

12 makers making,

11 fairies sparkling,
10 train cars chugging,
9 reindeer flying,
8 pirates playing,
7 robots dancing,
6 skaters skating,
5 donut rings . . .
4 mugs of cocoa,
3 shiny buttons,
2 Christmas stockings,
And some cookies for SANTA to eat.

The Plan:
Build ✓
Eat ✓
Play ✓
Stay up all night ✓
See Santa

MERRY
CHRISTMAS!

By Margaret Wang
Illustrated by AMEET Studio

AMEET Sp. z o.o.
Nowe Sady 6, 94-102 Łódź—Poland
ameet@ameet.eu
www.ameet.eu
www.LEGO.com

Published in the United States by Random House Children's Books, a division of Penguin Random House LLC, 1745 Broadway, New York, NY 10019, and in Canada by Penguin Random House Canada Limited, Toronto. Random House and the colophon are registered trademarks of Penguin Random House LLC.
rhcbooks.com
ISBN 978-0-593-43027-9 (trade) — ISBN 978-0-593-43063-7 (ebook)
Printed in the United States of America
10 9 8 7 6 5 4 3 2 1